DUCK TUNNEL

Story by Mary Risk

illustrations by The County Studio

HEINEMANN · LONDON

Joshua Jones and Spanner were loading bricks onto the *Delilah*. Spanner liked working the winch. He hooked the rope to a big drainpipe lying on the wharf, and cranked it up into the air.

"I didn't know Joe Laski wanted a drainpipe," said Josh. "I thought he only ordered bricks?"

"No," said Spanner. "I heard him say, 'bricks and a pipe'. He must have meant this drainpipe."

He pulled a lever on the winch, and the drainpipe whooshed through the air. Josh ducked. "Are you trying to knock me overboard, Spanner?" he yelled.

"Sorry," grinned Spanner.

Fiona had been watching Josh and Spanner.

"Are you going to the lock?" she said. "Can I come too?"

"Sure," said Josh. "Hop on board."

He untied the *Delilah's* mooring ropes, and cast off.

All kinds of little animals were running around in the spring sunshine. A squirrel was jumping about in the branches that overhung the canal, and some baby rabbits were peering out from the roots of a big old tree.

Fairport ran onto the roof of the *Delilah*, and stood looking down into the canal, barking loudly.

"What's the matter with him?" said Fiona.

She looked over the side. A family of ducklings was bobbing about on the water.

"Stop all that racket!" Josh said to Fairport. "You'll scare them silly!"

Down at the lock, no-one was around.

"Joe Laski isn't expecting us till dinnertime," said Josh.
"Let's go and find him."

They set off up the lane towards Laski's farm.

Joe was up by the pond. He was building a brick wall.

"Morning Joe," said Josh. "We've got your bricks for you."

"Very good," said Joe. "I bring the tractor down to the
lock. I give you helping hand to load them into the trailer."

Fiona was looking at the pond. So was Fairport.

"There's another family of ducklings, and their mum," she said. "No, Fairport. Don't you dare bark at them!"

"Five ducklings there are altogether," said Joe. "They are getting big now."

He got up and they all set off in the direction of the lock.

At the lock, Ravi had come out into the cottage garden.

"I saw the *Delilah*," he said to Josh. "I knew you'd be around somewhere. Have you brought something for Mr Laski?"

"Yes," said Joe. "Josh got bricks for my wall. You tell your grandad, maybe he let you come and see it."

Ravi ran into the cottage and out again.

"Bapu says I can come," he said.

"OK," said Joe, when the trailer was full. "We can go now."
"Hang on a minute," said Josh. "What about the drainpipe?"
"Drainpipe?" said Joe. "I don't want a drainpipe."
"That Spanner," said Josh. "I knew he was wrong. He said
you told him on the phone, you wanted bricks and a pipe."
"Pipe? No, I said 'pie'!" said Joe. "I wanted a pie from
Sharon's café for my dinner! Oh, never mind. We take the pipe
anyway. Maybe I find it useful somewhere."

"Look," said Fiona, when they got up to the pond, "the mother duck's got over Mr Laski's wall!"

"And where are all the ducklings?" said Ravi.

"Something's wrong," said Fiona. "The duck looks upset."

The mother duck kept flying up on to the wall, then peering down at the pond, and jumping off the wall on the other side.

Josh came by with a load of bricks.

"What's the matter with you two?" he said.

"It's the duck," said Ravi. "She's making a fuss, and we can't see the ducklings."

Josh looked at the duck, looked at the pond, and frowned.

"You know what?" he said. "She's trying to get them to the canal. They've got too big for the pond. There's not enough food for them here. Most years she just walks down to the canal and the ducklings all follow her. But now, the wall's in the way. She can fly over it, but the ducklings can't."

"That's awful!" said Fiona. "They're stuck!"

"You'll have to look for them," said Josh. "Then you can lift them over the wall and give them back to their mum."

"Right," said Fiona. "We'll get started."

Ravi saw the first duckling. It suddenly swam out from a clump of reeds, heard its mother calling, and got itself out of the water.

Very gently, Ravi picked it up, and handed it over the wall to Fiona, who put it down near its mother.

Fairport cocked his ears. He was watching everything.

Fiona saw the second duckling. It was trying to scramble over a big log. She took it back to its mum.

The third and fourth ducklings were easy to find. They were both right near the wall, under a big holly bush.

"It's all prickly in there," said Fiona. "Make a rustling noise, Ravi. Then they'll run out, and I can pick them up."

"Only one more to find," said Ravi, when the two ducklings were safely back with their mother.

They hunted high and low, under bushes, behind trees, and in the long grass, but they couldn't find it.

"I hope Fairport hasn't frightened it off," said Ravi.

"Where is Fairport, anyway?" said Fiona. "I haven't seen him for ages."

Ravi didn't answer. He'd found the last duckling.

"Look," he said. "He's climbed into the drainpipe."

The mother duck was quite calm now. She nudged her last lost duckling with her beak, then set off down the lane with her young family waddling along behind her.

"It'll take them ages to get to the canal," said Fiona. "Can't we carry them there, Josh?"

"No, leave them alone," said Josh. "The duck knows what she's doing. You'll upset her if you interfere."

"We soon finish unloading," said Joe. "Then we go down to the canal, see how mum and babies are getting on."

"Oh no!" cried Fiona suddenly. "Look!"

Fairport was trotting along with a duckling in his mouth!

"Fairport! You monster! How could you?"

Fiona was nearly crying.

"Drop it, Fairport," said Josh quietly.

But Fairport didn't drop the duckling. Instead he put it down, very gently. The duckling cheeped, and ran round looking for a hiding place.

"Clever dog! He hasn't hurt it at all!" said Ravi.

"Clever? He's daft!" said Josh. "He thought we were still hunting for ducklings. He didn't realize we wanted to leave them with their mother."

Fairport whined and thumped his tail.

"I'm sure he's saying sorry," said Fiona.

"He'd better be," said Josh. "Now, let's get this duckling back to the canal. You hold it, Ravi, and Fiona can hold Fairport. We don't want him being too helpful again!"

At the cottage, Admirable Karia was inspecting his
daffodils.

"No flopping about at the back there!" he was saying.

"Hello, Admirable," said Fiona. "Have you seen any ducks
come this way?"

"A large and thriving family passed only five minutes
ago," said the Admirable.

"Oh good," said Ravi. "Then this little one can go back
with its brothers and sisters."

He and Fiona went to the canal bank.

"There they are!" said Fiona.

The mother duck and her ducklings were happily dabbling and diving, picking up morsels to eat.

Ravi knelt down on the bank, opened his hands, and the duckling tumbled out and into the water.

"Can't he swim fast!" said Ravi.

"Just a minute," said Fiona. "I thought there were five of them. Now there are six. And look. That one Fairport brought is smaller than the others, and it's swimming on its own."

"Yes," said Ravi. "And the others are pushing it off."

"Mallard ducks only look after their own ducklings," said Fiona. "They'll chase strange ones away."

"Oh heck," said Ravi. "That means we've got a stray on our hands! We'll have to find its family."

"Josh . . . " said Fiona.

"I know," said Josh. "I heard. I suppose getting back to Biggott's will have to wait. We can't leave things like this!"

Josh, Ravi and Fiona started to search as the duck family made their way further down the canal.

Ravi looked up and down the canal.

"Its family could be anywhere!" he said. "If only Fairport . . . "

"Where *is* Fairport?" said Fiona. "He's disappeared again."

"Dratted dog," said Josh. "Don't worry, he'll be back."

"Josh," said Fiona, "perhaps this duckling comes from the family we saw on the way here. The ones Fairport barked at."

"Could be," said Josh. "Anyway, it's our only lead. We'd better walk back up the canal and see if we can spot anything."

There were lots of places along the canal bank where a family of ducks might be resting. Fiona and Ravi looked under every bush and in every crevice in the canal bank, and they were soon at the tunnel. All three of them peered into it.

"I thought I heard something," said Fiona.

"Me too," said Ravi.

"I can hear a sort of squeaking noise," said Ravi.

"And here comes the one who's making it!" said Fiona.

Out of the tunnel came a cross little duckling, cheeping furiously. Then came another, and another. Then came their mum, twisting her head round to see who was following her.

Next came another duckling, and last of all, Fairport. He was nudging the last duckling along with his nose to make it keep up with its mum.

"Fairport!" growled Josh. "Come here at once!"

Fairport swam over to the bank, climbed out and shook himself. A shower of water sprayed Josh, Fiona and Ravi.

"Hey!" shouted Ravi.

"Oi!" shouted Fiona.

"You daft great . . . " began Josh, but Fiona interrupted him.

"Josh, look!" she said.

The mother duck from the town side of the tunnel had seen
her lost duckling. It was a long way from the other family, still
trying to swim up the canal. Its mum gave a squawk, flapped
her wings, and half flew, half paddled along to it. All her other
babies bobbed along behind her, as fast as they could.

"Well," said Josh. "I reckon they'll be all right now.'

Fairport woofed softly. He was looking apologetic and pleased with himself at the same time.

"Daft dog thinks he sorted it out on his own," said Josh.

"Mission accomplished!" said the Admirable. "Women and children reunited!"

"Josh," said Joe, "I've had a good idea. You come up to the farm and I'll show you."

The drainpipe was still lying beside the new brick wall.

"Look," said Laski. "I dig a hole here, see?"

He dug the hole.

"And then I put the pipe like so, under the wall."

"Brilliant!" said Fiona. "Next year the duck can go through it, and the ducklings can follow her!"

"Spanner's not such a twit after all," said Josh. "His mix-up got the ducks their tunnel. Now come on Fi, we must go."

On board the *Delilah*, Fairport lay in the bows with his head on his paws.

"I reckon he's tired out," said Josh.

Fairport saw the baby rabbits again. He nearly stood up and barked, then just in time he stopped and looked up at Josh.

Josh took a hand off the wheel, and patted Fairport's head.

"That's more like it," he said. "Good old Fairport!"

William Heinemann Ltd, Michelin House,
81 Fulham Road, London SW3 6RB

LONDON MELBOURNE AUCKLAND

First published 1992 by William Heinemann Ltd
Joshua Jones film copyright © 1990 S4C
Joshua Jones character copyright © 1989 Rob Lee
Text copyright © 1992 William Heinemann Ltd
Illustrations copyright © 1992 William Heinemann Ltd
All rights reserved
Based on the animation series produced by
Bumper Films for S4C – Channel 4 Wales –
and Prism Art & Design Ltd

ISBN 434 94843 8

Produced by Mandarin
Printed in Hong Kong